Itsy-Bitsy's

Science Adventure

J. Douglas

Illustrated By: R. Simmons

On a beautiful day
after the rain went away,

ITSY-BITSY

took a walk.
He was lonely and wanted to talk.

Along the way, an **INSECT** stopped by. Landing on six legs, her name was Ms. **FLY**.

She had a lovely voice and started to sing, and then she was off, fluttering her wings.

Next, Itsy met a

SALAMANDER

named Willy,

and offered him a coat because it was chilly.

But Willy said, "I'm an AMPHIBIAN.

So, thanks, but I breathe through my skin."

That evening, they heard a noise
they hadn't heard before.

They ran off in that direction,
their interest growing more.
It was an auction on a nearby block.
"Do I have a bid? Eight mismatched socks!"

The **SPIDER** yelled,
"I'd like to make a bid!

"I have eight cold feet. I'm an
ARACHNID!"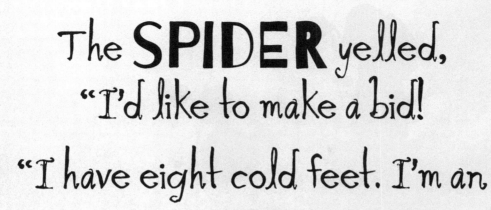

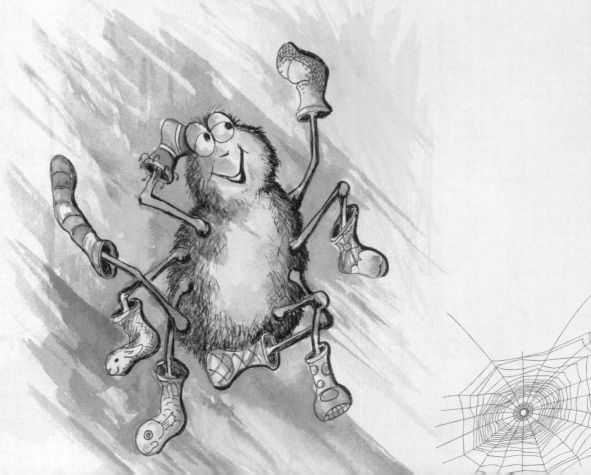

Itsy-Bitsy started walking home because it was getting dark.

He met Goldilocks and the

THREE BEARS

playing at a nearby park.

"What kind of animals are you?

INSECTS?
AMPHIBIANS?

Or something new?"

The bears laughed. "We'll tell you for sure.

We're called

MAMMALS

because of our fur!"

Goldilocks looked surprised.
"This is something we share!

HUMANS are
MAMMALS too,

but our 'fur' is called

'HAIR!'"

At the end of the day,
Itsy-Bitsy returned to his spout.
He sighed. "What a great day.
That's what

SCIENCE
IS ALL ABOUT."

ABOUT
THE AUTHOR

J. Douglas lives in Ontario, Canada with her husband and two young children. She has a Bachelor's degree in biology and has worked as an environmental consultant for the past ten years. Douglas has always loved science, bugs, microscopes, and playing in the dirt, and she wants to get children excited about science. She believes that science is all around us, and it isn't difficult to learn—but exciting to uncover!

All too often science isn't introduced until it's labeled as "too hard" or "uncool." Douglas' work showcases that science can be taught very young and that it doesn't need to be taught by a scientist.

ACKNOWLEDGEMENT AND DEDICATION

From J.D. –

Dedicated to my children – Make mistakes, be silly, be yourself and never stop learning and exploring. Do what makes you happy, I love you two with everything I've got.

To my husband and family – Thank you for the words of encouragement, feedback, and overwhelming support on this crazy adventure. I love you all.

To Coleen – without you, this book would not have happened. Thank you for your unwavering support, encouragement and love throughout the years.

Finally, I'd like to acknowledge the late "Dr. T." It is because of him that I have pursued a career and life in science.

From R.S. –

Dedicated to my two grandsons, Eli and Caleb, who mean the world to me.

◆ FriesenPress

Suite 300 - 990 Fort St
Victoria, BC, V8V 3K2
Canada

www.friesenpress.com

ISBN
978-1-5255-3191-0 (Hardcover)
978-1-5255-3192-7 (Paperback)
978-1-5255-3193-4 (eBook)

1. JUVENILE FICTION, ANIMALS

Distributed to the trade by The Ingram Book Company

ITSY-BITSY
Science Series

CPSIA information can be obtained
at www.ICGtesting.com
Printed in the USA
LVHW072123291118
598457LV00001B/2/P